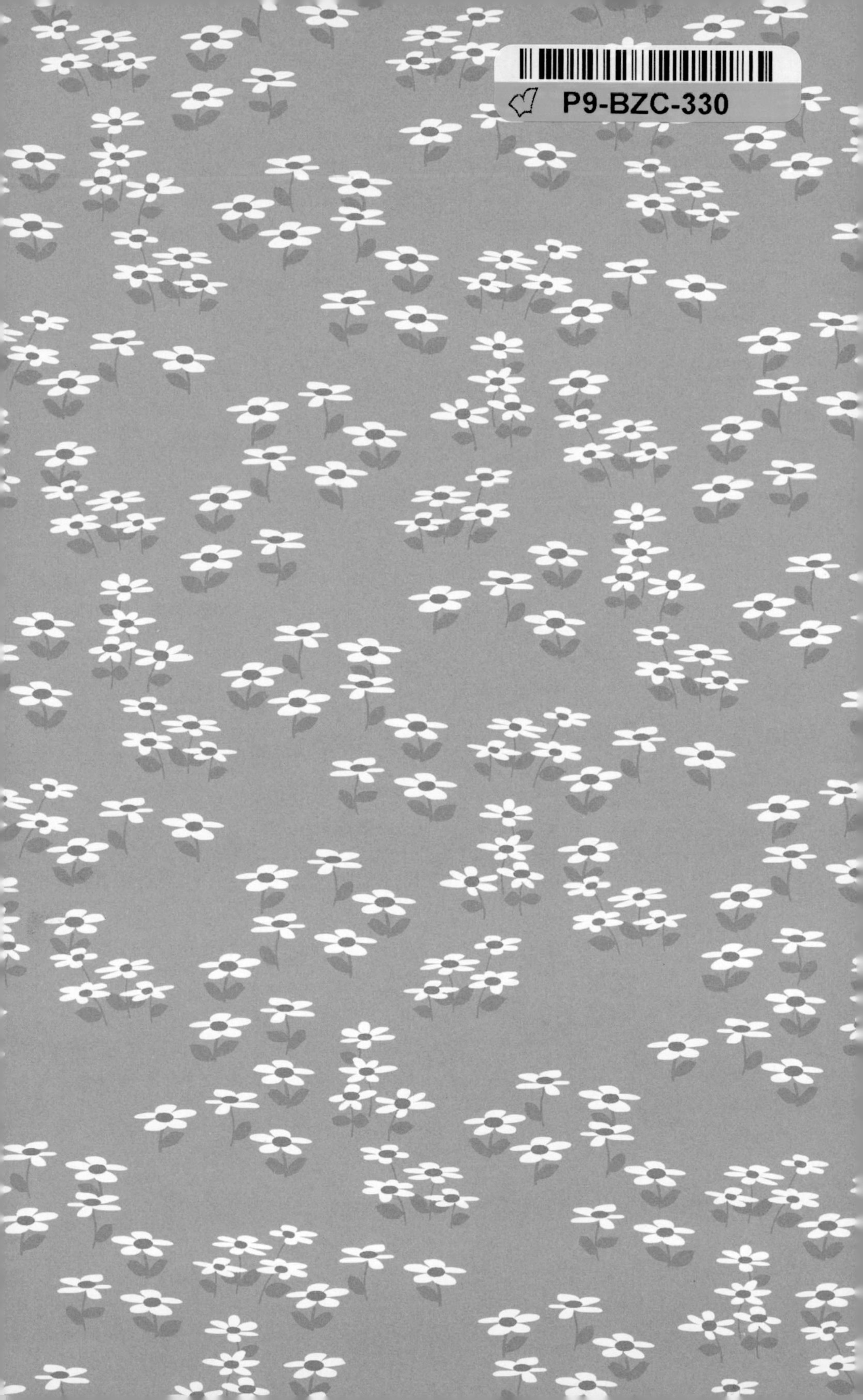
P9-BZC-330

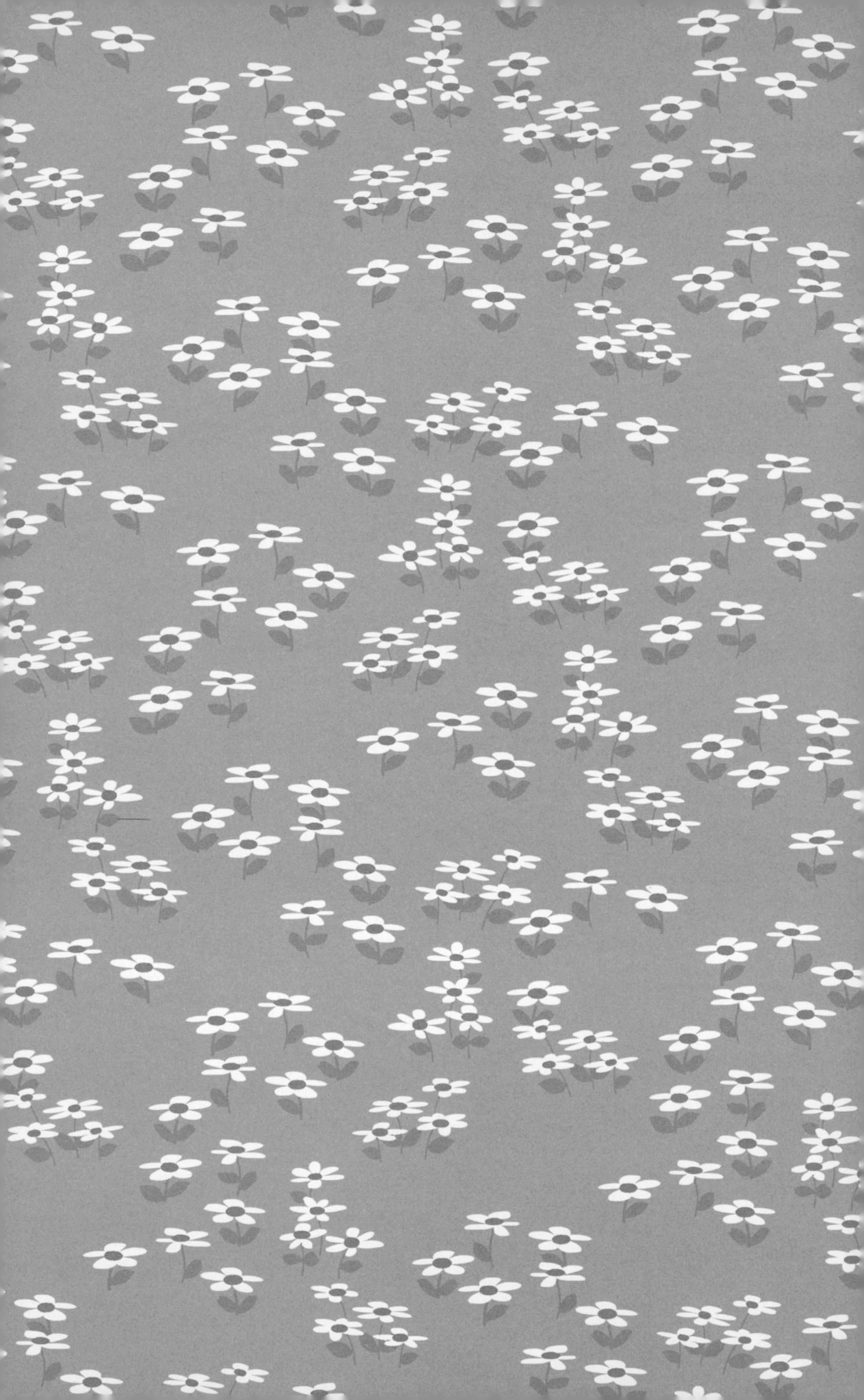

Monkey and Elephant Go Gadding

Monkey and Elephant Go Gadding

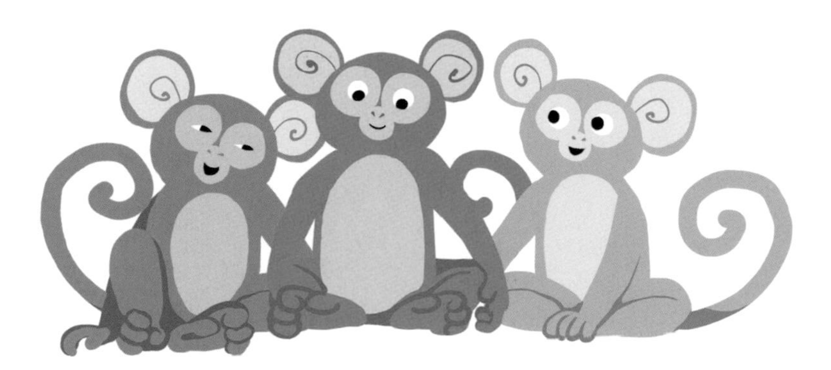

Carole Lexa Schaefer

illustrated by Galia Bernstein

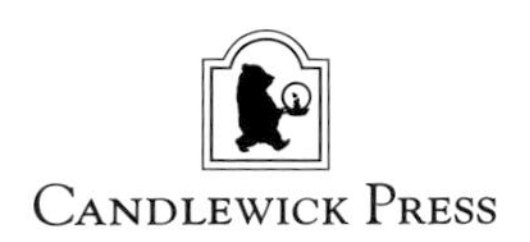

Candlewick Press

To a gifted gadder—Stefan, my grown-up Baby One

C. L. S.

For Haddar

G. B.

First edition 2014

Library of Congress Catalog Card Number pending
ISBN 978-0-7636-6128-1

13 14 15 16 17 18 CCP 10 9 8 7 6 5 4 3 2 1

Printed in Shenzhen, Guangdong, China

This book was typeset in Triplex.
The illustrations were created digitally.

Candlewick Press
99 Dover Street
Somerville, Massachusetts 02144

visit us at www.candlewick.com

Contents

Chapter One

STARTING OUT

Monkey washed her small, pink ears. Elephant washed his big, floppy ears. Monkey brushed her fur. She smiled. Elephant dusted his hide. He smiled.

"You look nice," said Elephant.

"You look nice, too,"

said Monkey.

"We both look very nice," said Elephant.

"Too nice to just stay home," said Monkey, twirling around.

"What should we do?" said Elephant, swishing his trunk.

Monkey scratched one clean ear. "Let's go gadding," she said.

"Gadding?" said Elephant. "What's that?"

"Gadding," said Monkey, "is

walking along,

looking around,

finding
something fun,
stopping awhile,

then moving on."

"Huh," said Elephant. "Maybe even finding a fun surprise?"

"Exactly," said Monkey. She turned three cartwheels. "Maybe more than one."

"Okay," said Elephant, lifting Monkey onto his head. "Let's go gadding!"

Chapter Two

FINDING UNCLE PHUMP

Monkey looked up. "I see lots of puffy clouds," she said.

Elephant looked down. "I see lots of footprints," he said.

"Way over there," said Monkey,
"I see lots of birds."

"Right here," said Elephant,
"I see a tall, grassy house."

"Ooh, let's stop,"
said Monkey.
"It could be fun."

"Okay," said Elephant. He swished his trunk against the door—*thump, thump.*

A tall, old elephant stepped out.

"It's Uncle Phump!" cried Elephant.

"It's young Elephant!" said Uncle Phump.

"Along with my friend, Monkey," said Elephant.

"You have a very nice house," said Monkey.

"It's my brand-new House for Making Hats," said Uncle Phump. "There's a hat here for everyone who stops by."

"Oh," said Elephant. "What a fun surprise!"

"I have never seen a house so full of hats," said Monkey, poking around.

Elephant tried on a tall, thin hat. Monkey climbed up and settled beside it.

"Just right," said Elephant.

"It is *your* hat," said Uncle Phump.

Monkey tried on a straw hat trimmed with red berries.

Elephant sniffed at the straw. "Yum," he said.

Monkey touched a berry. "Perfect for snack time," she said.

"Yes, if you like, you can eat *your* hat," said Uncle Phump. "And now, my dears, I must get back to work."

“Thank you, Uncle Phump,” said Monkey and Elephant together.

Elephant touched his hat with the tip of his trunk.

"Fun surprise number one!" he said.

"Yay!" Monkey cheered. "Isn't gadding great?"

Chapter Three

FINDING COUSIN MEEMEE

Monkey and Elephant walked along. They looked up. They looked down. They looked around.

Elephant looked at Monkey's straw hat.

"Gadding makes me hungry," he said.

Monkey touched the berries on her hat. "Gadding makes me hungry, too," she said. "Let's look for a nice place to have a snack."

"How about under that leafy tree?" said Elephant.

He set Monkey down. She turned a double somersault. "It's nice enough here for a fun surprise," she said.

A head popped out from between the leaves. "Did somebody say surprise?"

"It is Cousin MeeMee!" squealed Monkey.

"It is Cousin Monkey!" squealed MeeMee.

They danced around together.

More heads popped out from among the leaves.

"Meet my little family," said MeeMee. "Baby One, Baby Two, and Baby Three." The babies scrambled down the tree.

"My mama," said Baby One, pointing at Cousin MeeMee.

"Look at me," said Baby Two, pointing at himself.

"Hee-hee, funny," said Baby Three, laughing.

Monkey and Elephant opened their eyes very wide. The babies tumbled around them.

"Isn't this a fun surprise?" said Monkey.

"Um," said Elephant. "I think so."

"Will you join us for a swim?" asked MeeMee.

"Okay," said Elephant. He took off his hat.

"Sure, thanks," said Monkey. She took off her hat.

Monkey and Elephant splashed in the pond.

The babies splashed, too. "My pond," said Baby One.

"See me?" said Baby Two.

"Tee-hee-hee," said Baby Three,

laughing some more.

After a while, Monkey said, "Time for our snack."

"Yes," Elephant agreed.

Monkey and Elephant dried off. Elephant put on his hat. Monkey did not put on her hat. Where was it? She looked around.

The three babies were snoozing inside it. The red berries were all gone.

"Oh, my," said Monkey.

"Nap time for them," whispered Cousin MeeMee. "Snack time for us."

A nice snack was spread out under the tree.

"What a fun surprise!" said Monkey and Elephant together. "Thank you, Cousin MeeMee."

Elephant snacked on sweet hay cake. Monkey and MeeMee ate mashed-banana pie.

"Yum," said Monkey, rubbing her tummy.

"Yum," said Elephant, waving his trunk.

Monkey yawned. "Now it is *my* nap time," she said. "We must go."

"What about your hat?" asked Cousin MeeMee.

"The babies may keep it," said Monkey. "It fits them best."

"So it does," said MeeMee. "Come back soon."

"We will," said Monkey.

"Bye-bye," said Elephant. He lifted Monkey back onto his head.

The two friends set off for home—bump, galump.

"Well, Elephant," said Monkey, "did you like our day of fun surprises?"

"For sure!" said elephant.

Wah, wah, wah! he trumpeted.

"Gadding is great!"